HARRY POTTER

The Ultimate Book Of Facts

Unofficial & Unauthorised

Jack Goldstein & Frankie Taylor

First published in 2013
This edition published in 2017 by
Acorn Books
www.acornbooks.co.uk
an imprint of
Andrews UK Limited
www.andrewsuk.com

Contents

Through JK Rowling's books and films, we have been introduced to a fantastic and magical world that many of us would like to visit, despite the chance of running into a Death Eater or even Voldemort himself. If you love the world of Harry Potter, we really hope you'll enjoy reading this book!

Jack Goldstein & Frankie Taylor

HARRY POTTER
The Ultimate Book of Facts

Hogwarts

1. We are told that Hogwarts castle is 'somewhere in Scotland'. In the films, a real castle (Alnwick in Northumberland) is used for some external shots, although a model was used for many scenes – this explains why the castle looks so realistic – if it was mainly CGI, you would easily be able to tell!

2. You would think that a muggle might come across Hogwarts whilst walking around Scotland... this doesn't happen however as there are a whole host of charms and enchantments to keep prying eyes away. If a muggle does stumble across the school, all they will see are ruins and danger signs.

3. The eight core subjects taught at Hogwarts are *Astronomy, Charms, Defence against the Dark Arts, Flying, Herbology, History of Magic, Potions* and *Transfiguration*. From the third year onwards, students can also choose from these: *Arithmancy, Care of Magical Creatures, Divination, Muggle Studies* and *Study of Ancient Runes*. In the sixth year, students can choose to study *Alchemy* and *Apparition*. There are also eleven extra-curricular subjects offered: *Ancient Studies, Art, Earth Magic, Muggle Art, Music, Muggle Music, Ghoul Studies, Magical Theory, Xylomancy, Frog Choir* and *Hogwarts Orchestra*.

4. You might know that it was Helga Hufflepuff who brought the house elves to work at Hogwarts; despite Hermione's feelings this was in fact to give them a job where they wouldn't be abused. But did you know that much of the food made today is by recipes Helga gave to the house elves all those years ago?

5. In the books, the tallest of the Hogwarts towers is the astronomy tower. It is out of bounds – except for classes. According to Nearly-Headless Nick, the Bloody Baron 'likes to groan and clank' up it! In the *Half-Blood Prince* film however, it *isn't* the tallest tower and was even relocated (when compared to the books) to be over the transfiguration courtyard.

6. If you read the books and watch the films again, you might notice that the only electronic devices mentioned at Hogwarts are radios. There are no computers, televisions, iPads or anything else. This is because magic fields cause any equipment to go haywire around the grounds (at least this is what we are told by Hermione). So how come radios work? Easy – JK Rowling says they're powered by magic in the wizarding world, not electricity.

7. If you're not from Great Britain or Ireland, sadly you'll never be admitted to Hogwarts. It is exclusively for children from these two countries.

8. So, children come to Hogwarts from the age of eleven. You would expect magical children to attend a 'junior' wizards school, wouldn't you? Apparently not – most of them are home-schooled, however a few actually go to their local muggle junior school! I bet they have a hard time keeping their powers under wraps...

9. The Great Hall was one of the first sets made for the films. It took thirty men more than eighteen weeks to construct it from nearly 100 tonnes of plaster! The tables are an amazing 121 metres long and were of course made especially for the set. They are covered with graffiti from the Harry Potter actors, something that was actually encouraged by the set designer so that they had a more realistic look.

10. Hogwarts isn't left in the best condition after the battles in *The Deathly Hallows*. For the films, five massive truckloads of rubble (albeit made from polystyrene) were used in the various scenes!

Daniel / Harry

11. Daniel's full name is Daniel Jacob Radcliffe.

12. His father is a literary agent and his mother a casting agent.

13. Daniel has said he wasn't very good at school and found the work really difficult – although he did achieve three A grades!

14. Daniel's parents didn't tell him about the role for Harry Potter because the contract required shooting all seven films in Los Angeles and California.

15. Along with most of the cast, during the last day of filming Daniel openly wept.

16. Harry's full name is Harry James Potter.

17. It was decided that Harry was to be an orphan because he needed to be free from the fear of disappointing his parents.

18. Harry's pain and longing for his parents became much stronger than in initial drafts after J.K Rowling lost her mother in December 1990.

19. Harry's Birthday is on July 31st.

20. Unlike many other characters in the stories, Harry is not based on a real-life person.

The Malfoys

21.   Lucius Malfoy's father was named Abraxas Malfoy. In ancient Greece, the word abraxas was carved into amulets that also had pictures of basilisks on them – a real-life link to the chamber of secrets maybe! In addition to this, the word Abracadabra is supposedly related to the word Abraxas, with ancient peoples believing it had magical properties.

22.   The Malfoys, of course, claim to be a pure-blood family. According to Hagrid, there is no such thing anymore, however Lucius and his clan certainly wouldn't want you to think that! Being a pure-blood family in the Harry Potter universe can possibly be compared to pre-20th century European royalty. During this period of history, a member of the aristocracy from one country could only marry someone of similar stature from another. This led to a fair amount of inbreeding, which we now know is very bad for a human's genetic makeup (it causes all manner of health problems including ones of the mind). Perhaps this is what happened to the Malfoys and the Blacks...

23.   The Malfoy's family crest is black, green and silver and features images of a number of snakes and snake-like creatures. It bears the motto *Sanctimonia Vincet Semper* which translates as 'Purity Will Always Conquer'.

24. The first of the Malfoy family to set foot on English soil was a wizard called Armand Malfoy, who came over in 1066 during the Norman conquest. After helping William the Conqueror to win the country from the natives, the king awarded him the estate on which the family still live.

25. According to JK Rowling, Narcissa Malfoy was not actually a death eater, however she did agree with their pure-blood philosophy.

26. Rowling was very clever in choosing the name 'Malfoy'. In French it can be written as *Mal Foi* which translates as 'Bad Faith'. *Bad Faith* is in fact a concept in philosophy whereby an individual blames their failures on anyone (or anything) but themselves. This ties in perfectly with the actions of the characters throughout the books!

27. Emma Watson (who plays Hermione of course) has said that during filming – and despite rumours that circulated at the time, she never actually had a thing for Daniel Radcliffe. She did however have a major crush on Tom Felton, who plays Draco. We're not too sure Harry would approve of this...

28. JK Rowling has said that Draco Malfoy would have attended Durmstrang, which does not accept muggle-born wizards, however his mother didn't want him so far away from home... Ahhhhh!

29. Before settling on the name Malfoy, Rowling tried out other surnames including Spungen, Spinks and Smart.

30. The character of Lucius Malfoy is played by experienced actor Jason Isaacs. The two hosts of a BBC radio podcast – *Kermode & Mayo's Film Review* – are great fans of Jason, and in almost every one of their weekly shows announce 'Hello to Jason Isaacs'. This started a trend around the world where well-known TV programmes (amazingly even including a famous news channel) slipped the phrase into their broadcasts.

The Books

31. In *The Goblet of Fire*, there is a character called Natalie McDonald. A heart-warming story is behind her... Natalie was a real nine-year-old girl who was a huge Harry Potter fan. She had incurable leukaemia however, and knew she did not have long to live. Natalie wrote to JK Rowling to ask her what happened in the next book, but sadly by the time JK Rowling wrote back Natalie had died of her illness – so Rowling immortalised Natalie in the book.

32. JK Rowling's birthday is on the same day as Harry's.

33. There are more differences than you might think between the American and British versions of the books. Not only was 'Philosopher's Stone' changed to 'Sorcerer's Stone', but English phrases such as 'sneakers', 'jumper' and 'car park' were changed to 'trainers', 'sweater' and 'parking lot'.

34. Joanna 'JK' Rowling does not actually have a middle name – the 'K' is taken from her grandmother's name, Kathleen.

35. The books have been translated into more than 65 languages – including Latin!

36. Rowling got a number of the 'medieval' sounding words from Harry Potter (such as 'toadflax') from a famous real book written in the 1600s called *Culpepper's Complete Herbal.*

37. *Harry Potter and the Deathly Hallows* is the fastest-selling book of all time – 11 million copies were shifted on the day it was released.

38. On the day *The Prisoner of Azkaban* was released, Bloomsbury (the publisher) asked stores not to put the book on sale until schools closed – in a bid to stop children playing truant to buy it!

39. A handwritten copy of JK Rowling's *Tales of Beedle the Bard* sold for 4 million dollars!

40. More than 450 million Harry Potter books have been sold in total.

Emma / Hermione

41.   Emma's full name is Emma Charlotte Duerre Watson.

42.   After eight auditions and having only previously acted in school plays, she was cast to play Hermione Granger at the tender age of nine.

43.   Emma was nominated for five awards after her performance in *The Philosopher's Stone*.

44.   Emma starred in *The Queen's Handbag* – a mini edition of Harry Potter to celebrate Queen Elizabeth II's 80th birthday.

45.   In 2007, Emma – along with co-stars Daniel and Rupert – made imprints of their hands, feet and wands outside Grauman's Chinese Theater in Hollywood.

46.   Hermione's full name is Hermione Jean Granger.

47.   JK Rowling initially intended for her surname to be Puckle.

48.   Hermione's Parents are both dentists, which of course makes her muggle-born.

49. Rowling has said that Hermione's insecurities and fear of failure resemble herself at a young age.

50. The name Hermione is derived from Shakespeare's *The Winter's Tale*. JK Rowling wanted to give the character an unusual name so fewer girls could be teased over it.

The Ministry of Magic

51. The Ministry of Magic is a wizarding government in the United Kingdom responsible for regulating and enforcing laws for the magical community and also maintaining the community's identity from the muggle world.

52. A Minister for Magic is the main leader of the magical world and the highest ranking member of the Ministry. Many other wizarding countries also have ministers such as Bulgaria, Germany and New Zealand. The UK Minster of Magic plays a role similar to that of the Prime Minister.

53. There are seven departments within the Ministry, these are: The Department of Magical Law Enforcement, The Department of Magical Games and Sports, The Department of Magical Accidents and Catastrophes, The Department of Magical Transportation, The Department for the Regulation and Control of Magical Creatures, The Department of International Magical Cooperation and The Department of Mysteries.

54. The Ministry headquarters are located underground in the heart of London. Despite this, the ten-storey-high building has windows which reflect whatever weather magical maintenance wizards have chosen for the day.

55. The Minister for Magic has contact with the British Prime Minister via a wizard's portrait which can never be removed due to a permanent sticking charm. It is located in the Prime Minister's office at number ten Downing Street. The Ministry will only contact the PM if events in the magical world look to affect the muggle one.

56. One Minister for Magic that we're made aware of in the books is Millicent Bagnold who had previously attended Hogwarts and was sorted into Ravenclaw. It was she who was in power when James and Lily Potter were murdered. It is thought Millicent was in power between 1979-1990 which is the same time period as the UK's first female muggle Prime Minister – Margaret Thatcher.

57. After Millicent's retirement, the favourite for next Minister was Albus Dumbledore but he turned down the opportunity several times. Next in line was Bartemius Crouch Senior until his popularity took a huge hit when he sent his son to Azkaban. Third in line was Cornelius Oswald Fudge, former junior minister in the Department of Magical Accidents and Catastrophes.

58. After Fudge was forced to step down, Rufus Scrimgeour took his place... until Voldemort captured and tortured him. Refusing to talk, he was killed, just one year after being appointed. In the films, you may recognise his voice as that of Davy Jones from *Pirates of the Caribbean!*

59.   When the Death Eaters succeeded in taking over the Ministry, the Fountain of Magical Brethren (located in the atrium on level eight) was replaced with the 'Magic is Might' monument which showed a witch and wizard sitting on thrones with muggles twisted and pressed in a degrading way below them.

60.   After the destruction of Voldemort, Kingsley Shacklebolt became the last Minister of Magic that we know of. Kingsley led a huge reform which saw Ron and Harry in the Aurors' office and Hermione Granger fighting for the rights of non-humans and removing pro-pure-blood laws.

Death Eaters

61.   Alecto Carrow is one of only two confirmed female death eaters (the other of course being Bellatrix Lestrange). In the original Greek, Alecto means 'unceasing in anger', and in Greek Mythology Alecto was one of the *furies* who were vengeance personified and were cruel and bloodthirsty towards wrongdoers.

62.   There are twenty-four known Death eaters throughout the series – however, we can't be sure of the motives of every single one of them. Stan Shunpike for instance is most likely to have been under the imperius curse, as he is certainly not portrayed as a bad wizard. Regulus Black turned 'to the good side' after finding out about Voldemort's horcruxes, and Draco Malfoy did defect in the end – a little like Karkaroff, who fought alongside Voldemort in the first wizarding war, but didn't return after Voldemort's return. Whether this was down to fear or ethics however is not ascertained!

63.   Although Fenrir Greyback was permitted to attend all the Death Eater 'events' and was an important member of Voldemort's circle, he was in fact not a death eater himself, being a werewolf.

64. Wormtail is actually the only Death Eater who attended Hogwarts and wasn't in Slytherin. Strangely, considering the normal qualities shown by the students, he was sorted into Gryffindor.

65. Augustus Rookwood is strangely called Algernon Rookwood in *The Order of the Phoenix*, a fact which is never explained. Interestingly, Rookwood is the surname of one of the Gunpowder plot conspirators in English history.

66. In the *Goblet of Fire* film, we see Barty Crouch junior licking his lips (and later 'Moody' doing the same thing, revealing his identity). This action is not mentioned in the book, and was in fact first improvised by actor David Tennant.

67. There is an official Harry Potter t-shirt which features a 'wanted' poster of Bellatrix Lestrange, saying that she was convicted of murder. However, in the books, she was in fact sent to Azkaban not for murder but for torture – of Alice and Frank Longbottom of course.

68. There are interesting similarities between Wormtail (Peter Pettigrew/Scabbers) in Harry Potter and Grima Wormtongue in *Lord of the Rings*. They are both referred to most commonly by their 'worm' names; they are pathetic, cowardly people, and they both serve horrible masters who treat them poorly.

69. If you read the books particularly carefully, you will see that Macnair is sometimes spelt McNair – this is corrected in more recent reprints.

70. Death Eaters were originally called Knights of Walpurgis. Amazingly, there is a real night – the 30th April – which is called Walpurgis night. In times gone by it was this night – rather than Hallowe'en – when witches and demons were believed to have gathered!

The Films

71. *The Prisoner of Azkaban* was the lowest grossing film of the Harry Potter series – however it still made more than the highest grossing *Twilight* film!

72. Steven Spielberg was approached to direct the first Harry Potter film – but he wanted to make it as a Pixar-style animated movie.

73. During filming, Daniel Radcliffe wore out almost 70 wands; he also went through 160 pairs of glasses.

74. The brooms in the films are actually made from lightweight aluminium.

75. Warwick Davis actually played two roles in the Harry Potter films – Professor Flitwick in the first four films, and Griphook in The Deathly Hallows.

76. The twins who play Fred and George (James and Oliver Phelps) *aren't* actually redheads.

77. The films have taken a total of around eight *BILLION* dollars at cinemas worldwide.

78.   The biggest grossing film was the last one – *The Deathly Hallows part II*. It took almost $1.4 billion at the box office.

79.   The films were all shot at Leavesden Studios in England. Of course, there have also been many other locations used, such as Gloucester Cathedral for some outside scenes, and an Oxford University dining hall.

80.   Despite the fact that the films often differ in some significant ways to the books, JK Rowling actually helped write the scripts of all of the films. Apart from the fifth movie, they were all scripted by Steve Kloves (Michael Goldenberg wrote the screenplay for *Order of the Phoenix*).

Rupert / Ron

81.   Rupert's full name is Rupert Alexander Lloyd Grint.

82.   Amazingly, he owns an ice cream truck!

83.   Similar to his large family in Harry Potter, Rupert is the eldest of five children.

84.   Rupert joined a local theatre school and was cast as a fish in *Noah's Ark* and a donkey in another play.

85.   Like his co-star Emma Watson, Rupert had never acted professionally before Harry Potter.

86.   Ronald's full name is Ronald Bilius Weasley.

87.   Although not intended at the start, Ron is inspired by J.K Rowling's best friend.

88.   Ron's insecurities stem from a number of factors, those being: he is not an excellent quidditch player nor a noteworthy study, he was not the daughter his mother always dreamt of and often although not purposefully he is overshadowed by Harry's fame.

89. Before Ron begins his adult life working as an Auror in the Ministry of Magic, he joins Fred and George at Weasleys' Wizard Wheezes, a shop which becomes a huge success.

90. In the final instalment Ron and Hermione are married with two children called Rose and Hugo.

General Facts

91. *The New England Journal of Medicine* published an article that explained a new health issue whereby children were getting migraines from reading for unusually long periods of time. The physician who wrote the article called it 'Hogwarts Headache'.

92. Over 15,000 boys auditioned for the part of Harry Potter.

93. When Harry Potter was translated into Spanish, Neville's toad was accidentally called a turtle!

94. If you look carefully at the credits at the end of *Goblet of Fire*, you'll see the phrase 'No dragons were harmed in the making of this movie.'

95. When they were filming *The Prisoner of Azkaban,* the crew sewed Tom Felton's pockets shut – because he kept sneaking food onto the set!

96. Ron is well known for using expletives – but originally he was even more foul-mouthed! The publishers had to get JK Rowling to tone down his language as it would not have been appropriate for younger readers.

97.   Did you notice that Harry arrives at the Dursley's for the first time with Hagrid on the back of Sirius Black's motorbike – and leaves for the last time in exactly the same way?

98.   In the films, you always see Bellatrix standing on the right side of Voldemort – this is because being stood to the right hand side symbolises one's most loyal follower.

99.   The Marauders died in the exact opposite order as to how their names are printed on the map.

100. If you translate *Expecto Patronum* from Latin, it means 'I await a guardian'.

Ralph and Voldemort

101. Ralph's full name is – amazingly – Ralph Twisleton Wykeham Fiennes.

102. When he was asked to play Voldemort, Ralph had to admit that he hadn't actually read any of the books.

103. Ralph has compared Voldemort to a character from *Chitty Chitty Bang Bang*, saying that The Child Catcher was the literary figure he was most scared of when he was young.

104. Ralph said in one interview that during filming (when he was in full costume), he walked past the child of a script supervisor. The child burst into tears. Ralph says this made him feel good about himself...!

105. Ralph also once said that he understands Voldemort's evilness, saying that being very lonely as a child probably contributed to his character.

106. According to JK Rowling, you don't pronounce the 'T' at the end of Voldemor*T*.

107. Voldemort's real name is of course Tom Marvolo Riddle.

108. Voldemort has in fact been played by six different actors in the films. Ian Hart and Richard Bremner both played him in different scenes in the first film. Christian Coulson played Tom Riddle in *The Chamber of Secrets.* Ralph Fiennes is obviously best-known for the role, but Hero Fiennes-Tiffin (Ralph's nephew) played the young Tom Riddle in *Half-blood Prince,* and Frank Dillane played him in the same film as an adolescent.

109. Voldemort cannot understand love as he was conceived when his father was under the influence of a love potion – something known in the wizarding world to cause emotional complications.

110. One ability that Voldemort possesses that amazes even the most worldly-wise of wizards is that he can fly without the aid of any magical instrument.

Differences

111. In the books, Hagrid is said to be twice as tall as a regular human being, making him around 11 to 12 feet high – however, in the films it is referenced that he is 'only' 8 foot 6.

112. Peeves the poltergeist has appeared in every single Harry Potter book – and none of the films at all. Rik Mayall did film some scenes as Peeves for the first film, but they didn't make it into the final cut.

113. In the film of *The Deathly Hallows*, Hermione is seen obliviating her parents – this isn't mentioned at all in the book. Many critics have said this was a fantastic thing for the film to feature however, as it sets the tone of the final chapter (or two) in the Harry Potter series.

114. Many fans were disappointed that the films did not feature the sequence where Luna Lovegood is commentator for a Quidditch match, and rather than talking about the game starts pointing out interestingly shaped clouds – amongst other hilarious things!

115. In the first film, the name of Harry's Owl (Hedwig) is *NEVER* mentioned.

116. In the books, Dudley eventually redeems himself, and he sees the error of his ways. In the films however, the last we see of Dudley is him escaping with the rest of the Dursleys. This was a real shame for many, as the way it was originally written showed that even the worst bullies could change.

117. Hermione's SPEW – the society for the Promotion of Elfish Welfare – is not mentioned in the films at all, yet features quite heavily in some books – particularly *The Goblet of Fire* and *The Deathly Hallows*.

118. Although it is explained in the book, the film *Harry Potter and the Half-blood Prince* never actually explains exactly why Snape called himself this. Seriously – watch the film again if you don't believe us!

119. In the books, Hermione is described as having huge front teeth and frizzy hair. Most people would agree this isn't exactly an accurate description of Emma Watson!

120. Most of this section has been about things that are in the books but not in the films. But did you notice that in the Knight Bus there is a talking shrunken head – this isn't in the books at all, and JK Rowling has said she wishes she'd thought of it!

Other Characters

121. JK Rowling didn't actually make up the word 'Dumbledore' – it is an early English word for 'Bumblebee'.

122. Moaning Myrtle is technically a little old to be a schoolgirl – the actress who played her was 37 years old at the time!

123. Pansy Parkinson is based on real-life bullies who tormented Jo Rowling when she was younger.

124. People believe Hermione's cat Crookshanks to be part kneazle – a kneazle is like a cat but with big ears and a tail similar to a lion's.

125. Fred and George celebrate their birthdays on April Fool's Day. Who would have guessed!

126. In the *Chamber of Secrets* film, Dumbledore has a portrait on his wall of Gandalf the Grey from *Lord of the Rings!*

127. In *The Half-Blood Prince,* the Gryffindor chaser is called Demelza Robins. She is named after Daniel Radcliffe's favourite charity – the Demelza House Children's Hospice.

128. Although Griphook was played by Warwick Davis in *The Deathly Hallows*, the character was played by Verne Troyer (Mini Me from Austin Powers) in the first film – but they still used Warwick's voice!

129. In the final scene of the last film, Draco Malfoy's wife is actually played by Tom Felton's real-life girlfriend Jade Olivia.

130. James Potter was a chaser and not a seeker.

Dumbledore

131. Do you know Dumbledore's full name (including post-nominal letters)? If you do you must have a fantastic memory! It is Professor Albus Percival Wulfric Brian Dumbledore, Order of Merlin, First Class, Grand Sorc., D. Wiz., X.J. (sorc.), S. of Mag. Q!

132. Before he became headmaster, Dumbledore was the professor of transfiguration. He has also held other posts, including Chief Warlock of the Wizengamot and Supreme Mugwump of the International Confederation of Wizards.

133. Perhaps unsurprisingly, when Dumbledore attended Hogwarts he was sorted into Gryffindor house. His first term at the school was in the autumn of 1892, and on his first day became friends with Elphias Doge. No-one else wanted to get acquainted with Doge because he was suffering from a bad case of dragon pox!

134. During his time at the school, he was pretty much a perfect student. He did however once set the curtains of his dormitory on fire 'by accident'... he said he hadn't liked them anyway!

135. What terrible thing does Dumbledore see a Boggart as? Sadly it is the corpse of his sister, Ariana.

136. It is often mentioned that the post of defence against the dark arts teacher is cursed. This is in fact true! The curse was put on the post by Lord Voldemort when Dumbledore turned him down for the job when he applied (for the second time – he had already been turned down by Armando Dippet, the previous headmaster). Dumbledore rightly suspected Voldemort had been carrying out illicit activities and therefore didn't want him in a position of power in his school. This didn't go down too well with Voldemort...

137. The character of Dumbledore was played in the first two films by Richard Harris. Sadly however, Harris died after filming *The Chamber of Secrets*, so the role was then given to Michael Gambon. But a third actor has also played the great wizard – Toby Regbo. If that name doesn't ring any bells, you can be forgiven – he played a very young Dumbledore in *The Deathly Hallows Part One*.

138. Richard Harris knew his health was on the wane when he accepted the role. He did so reluctantly, knowing he would probably not live to play Dumbledore throughout the whole series. The reason he took the job on was because his granddaughter (who was aged eleven at the time) threatened never to speak to him again if he didn't take it!

139. Apparently, one of Dumbledore's greatest achievements was discovering the twelve uses of dragon blood. The only one we're actually *told* of is simply that it is a fantastic oven cleaner.

140. If you think of other great film wizards, one of the first that probably comes to mind is that of Gandalf in the *Lord of the Rings* series. Gandalf was played by Sir Ian McKellen, who was actually offered Dumbledore's role after Harris died. Yet he turned it down for two specific reasons. Firstly, he felt it was too similar to his most famous fantasy Tolkien-based outing; secondly – and rather amusingly – because Harris had called him a 'dreadful actor' before his death!

Quidditch

141. A quidditch pitch is bigger than you might think –
certainly length-wise at least. It is an oval shape, at its
furthest points five hundred feet long and one hundred
and eighty feet wide; that's about 150 by 55 metres.
Compare that to a football (soccer) pitch, which is
between 90 and 120 metres long and from 45 to 90
metres wide.

142. There was once a quidditch team called the *Banchory
Bangers*, but most wizards haven't heard of them. This
is because they were disbanded by the Department of
Magical Games and Sports because they repeatedly
broke the rules set down by The International Statute of
Wizarding Secrecy of 1692. Mainly, the team did not play
their quidditch matches far enough away from Muggle
towns.

143. In most sports that are enjoyed across the world,
substitutions are commonplace. Not so in quidditch!
Would you believe that no matter how injured a player
is, they are *not allowed* to be replaced?! Strangely, one
passage in the book of *The Goblet of Fire* seems to dispute
this fact, as an instance is mentioned where a game went
on for many days and the players had to be switched
as they were 'too tired to carry on'. Perhaps there was a
special exception in this case!

144. The official magazine about quidditch in the wizarding world is called *Seeker Weekly*.

145. The beautiful continent of Africa boasts four quidditch teams about which we are told: the *Gimbi Giant-Slayers* from Ethiopia, the *Patonga Proudsticks* from Uganda, the *Sumbawanga Sunrays* from Tanzania and the *Tchamba Charmers* from Togo.

146. How did quidditch get its name? The first recorded game took place at Queerditch Marsh. We know this because a witch called Gertie Keddle who lived near the marsh recorded what she saw in a diary, which survives to this day!

147. Some people just can't get enough quidditch from reading the Harry Potter books and watching the films... They actually play it! Muggle quidditch (as it is known) was apparently created in 2005 at Middlebury College in Vermont, and is supposedly as close as one can get to the sport the JK Rowling invented – but (unsurprisingly) without magic broomsticks! The first muggle quidditch world cup took place in March 2013, and featured an incredible 56 teams from four different countries.

148. If you're wondering how this muggle version of the sport handles the snitch... well, someone dresses up in bright yellow and hides somewhere on the campus grounds where the game is taking place. The seekers then have to find them. It is basically an enormous game of hide and seek!

149. If you love quidditch but are not overly convinced that the Muggle version would be as fun as the wizarding one, you might want to dig that old games console out of your parents' attic... EA Games released *Harry Potter Quidditch World Cup* on the original Xbox (and PS2 amongst other platforms). If you're lucky, you might be able to pick up a copy from eBay!

150. There are seven hundred types of foul in quidditch, however ten are listed as the most common. Can you name all of them? They are *blagging, blatching, blurting, bumphing, cobbing, flacking, haversacking, quaffle-pocking, snitchnip* and *stooging*. An interesting note about fouls – in the 1473 world cup final, all seven hundred types of foul were committed in just the one game. These included such unusual methods of play as the transfiguring of a chaser into a polecat and the release of one hundred blood-sucking vampire bats from under the Transylvanian captain's robes!

The Weasleys

151. In the 1930s, a directory of pure-blood wizards was published and featured something called the 'Sacred Twenty-Eight'. This was twenty-eight families who were still *truly* pure-blood at the time. The Weasleys were not happy with their inclusion on this list, and claimed that their ancestors actually had ties with a number of interesting muggles!

152. It was Arthur Weasley himself who bewitched the car (a light blue Ford Anglia 105E Deluxe) first featured in *The Chamber of Secrets*. The question is, how did he not fall foul of the law regarding misuse of Muggle artefacts? Well, Arthur Weasley actually wrote the law, and included a loophole which meant it would still be legal if he didn't *actually intend* to fly the car!

153. Molly's name was used as it is a part of the word 'mollycoddle' which means to overprotect something or someone. You'd probably agree that this is a very good way to describe the matriarch of the Weasley household!

154. JK Rowling chose Molly to kill Bellatrix Lestrange as she wanted to show that despite dedicating her life to her household and family, Molly was still a powerful witch – a positive role model for all homemakers.

155. In *The Order of the Phoenix*, Rowling originally intended that Arthur would be killed by Nagini – however she backed out of this at the last minute. This was because she felt that he is one of the few 'good' fathers in the series, and therefore needed to stay in the latter books.

156. On the subject of the twins' joke shop, if you only watched the films there is something pretty major that isn't explained... how they got the money to make their business take off in the first place! Of course, in the books, Harry gives Fred and George his winnings from the Triwizard tournament. But this doesn't happen in the *Goblet of Fire* film!

157. Have you noticed how many of the Weasley family have names from Medieval times, with particular reference to the legend of King Arthur? There is *Arthur* himself of course, *Percy* from Sir Percival (one of the knights of the round table), *Charles* (from Charlemagne, a medieval king), *Fred* from Frederick Barbaross (an emperor who took part in the crusades). Amazingly, King Arthur's spear was called Rhongomyniad, but was shortened to *Ron* by Geoffrey of Monmouth. And lastly, Ginny's full first name is *Ginevra*, which is the Italian name for *Guinevere* – and Guinevere was King Arthur's Queen!

158. For Rupert Grint's audition, he dressed up like his female drama teacher, and rapped about Ron Weasley. The words went like this: 'Hello, my name is Rupert Grint, I hope you don't think I stink.' Amazingly as you'll know, he still got the part...

159. Here's an example of a scene where different things happen depending on what you're watching, reading or playing... In the *Goblet of Fire* film, when Fleur says goodbye to Ron, she kisses him on the forehead. In the book she doesn't do anything special. And in the computer game, she slaps him on the cheek!

160. In medieval times in the real world, having ginger hair was actually considered a surefire sign of witchcraft!

Muggles

161. JK Rowling used the word 'Muggle' as it is similar to the word 'mug', which means a gullible person. However, she added the extra syllable so it was a little bit softer, therefore showing that wizards didn't use the word 'muggle' as an offensive term. However, when Harry Potter was translated into Brazilian, the word muggle became *trouxa*, which in English actually means fool!

162. Although she has never visited it, Rowling got the name 'Dursley' from a town in Gloucestershire – purely because she liked the sound of it!

163. Petunia Dursley is not a particularly nice muggle. The way she treats Harry is quite awful, and she has spoken of her jealousy of her sister Lily... no surprise then that in real life, the petunia flower actually symbolises resentment and anger.

164. Originally, Hermione was going to have a younger sister who was a muggle – but for currently unknown reasons, JK Rowling decided *not* to proceed with her character.

165. You know the name of Harry's parents; you know the name of Ron's. But what about Hermione's? We're told they're dentists of course, but their first names? They're never mentioned in the main series of books or the films!

166. In the books, only five characters have their thoughts and not just their actions portrayed by the author. Three of these are muggles – Vernon Dursley, the British Prime Minister and Frank Bryce. The non-muggles are Narcissa and of course Harry himself.

167. If you pay attention whilst watching *the Deathly Hallows Part 1*, during the scene set in Umbridge's office at the Ministry of Magic, you'll see a book by Barrett Fay called *When Muggles Attack*. Fay also wrote a book titled *Mudbloods and How to Spot them*. Not a particularly nice wizard!

168. According to JK Rowling's official site, a wizard called Hambledon Quince once wrote a controversial document which proposed the theory that muggles originated from mushrooms!

169. The Gameboy Colour version of the *Chamber of Secrets* game is genuinely a bit strange. That particular version goes out of its way never to mention the word 'muggle'. Even muggle studies in the game are renamed to 'non-magical studies'. Nintendo have never explained their reasoning for this!

170. Rowling has admitted that at first she wrote a section about Dudley Dursley in the epilogue of the final book – where he actually turns up at platform nine and three quarters with his own magical child! She eventually erased this, as she felt it would be unrealistic – the reason being that no latent magical genes could ever have survived contact with Vernon Dursley's DNA!

The Triwizard Tournament

171. The tournament is a magical contest held between three of the largest wizarding schools of Europe. These are *Hogwarts, the Durmstrang Institute* and *Beauxbatons Academy of Magic.*

172. The competition, set to take place every five years, is renowned for being highly dangerous and is thought to have begun as early as 1294. In 1972 however, it was cancelled due to a number of deaths – but was later revived once safer measures had supposedly been put into place.

173. Cedric Diggory and Fleur Delacour both used the *bubble-head charm* during the second task in the tournament, enabling them to breath underwater. In real life, Robert Pattinson spent around two months preparing for this particular scene. A whole three weeks of this were actually spent learning to scuba dive!

174. Daniel revealed he spent a total of forty-one hours and thirty-eight minutes underwater in order to film the second task.

175. The maze in the film was very different to that in the book. Did you notice a distinct lack of boggarts, sphinxes, acromantulas and blast-ended skrewts?!

176. Another 'spot the difference' moment... In the *Goblet of Fire* film, we see Neville Longbottom giving Harry the gillyweed needed for his second task in the Triwizard Tournament. However, in the book we're told Harry in fact receives the gillyweed from Dobby.

177. When the two other contending schools arrive at Hogwarts, the books tell us it was Friday 30th October, and we can deduce it would have been 1994. If we take a look back at a real-life diary however, the 30th October 1994 was actually a Sunday!

178. During the underwater filming, Daniel Radcliffe and other cast and crew members took a photo which he later sent out as a Christmas card with photoshopped antlers and red noses on everyone's faces!

179. JK Rowling initially wanted the Triwizard tasks to focus around the elements of earth, air, fire and water but finding one for each proved too difficult – so fire and air were combined, resulting in the trial of the dragons.

180. The Yule Ball is held on Christmas Day night – the evening of Yule, a traditional winter festival celebrated in northern Europe also referred to as Christmas.

The Most Amazing Facts

181. What's the name of the train that travels from platform nine and three quarters? If you said *the Hogwarts Express,* you'd actually be wrong. It is in fact called *the Hogwarts Castle.* Hogwarts Express is the name of the *route* that the train follows! In real life, the train used was built in 1937 (two years before the second world war started), and it pulls four carriages from the 1950s.

182. In the *Goblet of Fire* film, Professor Snape is shown at the Yule Ball, although according to the book he never actually attended.

183. Would you agree that Weasleys' Wizard Wheezes looked absolutely fantastic in the films, and amazingly realistic for what in reality would be impossible products? The graphic designer for the films (Eduardo Lima) actually created 300 names for Weasley products just so they could be made, and they *all* feature in the background of the shop scenes. What an amazing amount of detail!

184. The character of Marjorie Dursley (Vernon's sister who is 'inflated' by Harry in *The Prisoner of Azkaban*) was actually based on a real person – JK Rowling's grandmother!

185. The first time we see Death Eaters in the film series, they have particularly pointy hoods. The costumes were changed to remove this feature from later films though, as some commentators noticed an unnerving similarity between the initial look used for Voldemort's followers and despicable racist group the Ku Klux Klan. Of course, one could say that the comparisons don't stop there...

186. JK Rowling has said that Dementors are the embodiment of depression – a disease that she has suffered with at various times during her life.

187. Although the films don't mention Hermione's obsession with 'saving' the house-elves from what she sees as their enslavement, the books consider this a key point of her character. However, the book she refers to on a huge number of occasions – *Hogwarts: A History* – doesn't mention that house elves are used to prepare the food and conduct other menial tasks. This, of course, annoys Hermione so much that she suggests the book should be renamed... *A Highly Biased and Selective History of Hogwarts Which Glosses Over the Nastier Aspects of the School* is one of her suggestions!

188. Daniel Radcliffe's stunt double throughout the films is called David Holmes. David is sadly now wheelchair bound, after a stunt filmed for *The Deathly Hallows* went tragically wrong.

189. Once during filming, a real fruit bat got stuck in Hagrid actor Robbie Coltrane's beard!

190. Despite JK Rowling almost going out of her way to ensure that religion is *not* mentioned or discussed in any of the Harry Potter books, some Christians and Muslims have accused the series of containing occult and satanic subtexts. Sadly, some people have protested the books' inclusion in libraries in America on the basis that they promote 'real-life' magic and various forms of evil.

191. It was in fact a Christian priest named Father Gabriele Amorth who said that reading Harry Potter is 'Satanic' and 'leads to evil'. Amazingly, he was at the time the Vatican's *Chief Exorcist!*

192. Kings Cross Station actually now has a plaque that says 'Platform 9 3/4' and is a popular spot for London tourists to take selfies.

193. JK Rowling originally called the Death Eaters the 'Knights of Walpurgis'.

194. When JK Rowling took an online sorting hat quiz, she was placed into Hufflepuff.

195. Before people in England thought that witches and wizards flew on Broomsticks – like in Harry Potter – they actually thought they flew whilst sitting inside cauldrons!

196. When Arthur Weasley has to enter a number into the telephone box to get into the Ministry of Magic, he dials '62442'. Press the buttons on your cellphone spelling the word 'Magic' and see what you get...

197. The four houses of Hogwarts are supposed to represent the four classical elements – with Gryffindor being fire, Ravenclaw air, Hufflepuff earth and Slytherin water.

198. After filming *The Order of the Phoenix*, Emma Watson nearly decided to quit the franchise – however (and we're all glad about this) – she decided to stay as the 'pluses outweighed the minuses'.

199. There are rumours that JK Rowling isn't finished with Harry Potter just yet – although no-one can say what age Harry would be if she does write another book...

200. JK Rowling is the only person in the entire history of humankind who has ever become a billionaire by writing a book!

And Finally...

201. Michael Jackson asked if he could make a stage musical of the Harry Potter series, but JK Rowling wouldn't allow him to do it.

You may also enjoy...

JACK GOLDSTEIN & FRANKIE TAYLOR

HARRY POTTER

THE COMPLETE
QUIZ BOOK

UNOFFICIAL & UNAUTHORISED

CPSIA information can be obtained
at www.ICGtesting.com
Printed in the USA
BVOW10s0524261117
500832BV00002B/13/P